2

The Truth About Boo

By

Peggy Mercer

Published by Peggy Mercer

Worldwide

Credits

The Truth About Boo is a children's book for ages 6-10, or grades pre-K through 5th. The book is an easy reader and especially a book for October spotlighting Halloween.

Published by Peggy Mercer Worldwide Media, 988 Estlee Mercer Road, Douglas, Georgia 31535.

All rights reserved. No part of this story may be copied, used, streamed, or quoted without permission of the author. World rights protected under International Copyright and Pan American Copyright laws.

© Peggy Mercer, October 2021

Dedication

For dear niece, Shannon and her husband, Jon, and my great niece, Chloe, who love all things Halloween, and in honor of their precious Raven.

Acknowledgements

I wish to thank my niece, Shannon and my great niece, and Jon Smith for their help with the story of Boo. We all grew up loving Halloween and Shannon provided photos and input as did Chloe. I also thank Brenda Finch for the photos of Big Daddy's old tractor that once caught fire but is so meaningful.

I also thank my readers, who push push, pushed me to do this Halloween story. They love this spooktacular time of year called Halloween.

Author's Note:

During the several years past, our children have had a hard time adjusting to no school, less parties, less activities, masks, no masks, confusing times. And yet, they have continued to read, and their parents have continued to share books with them and stories which lift their hearts and make them laugh.

If it my joy and an honor to continue to share stories I am blessed to write, with children. May God bless you all as we continue to read, to learn, to feel good and to lift our eyes toward the horizon of better times ahead.

This is Boo, welcome to my story!

The Truth About Boo

Peggy Mercer

Introduction

Down an old dirt road in the deep South, farmhouses are here and yonder. One house is in a field, surrounded by tall pine trees and on one side a pond, full of fish and turtles.

There is a dock on the pond, a barn, dirt yards where grass won't grow because chickens roam free as the breeze and will peck out your eyes, much less every blade of grass. So…no, there is no grass in the yard.

This is where BOO lives. Boo is a cat, but no ordinary cat.

Boo is a black Scaredy Cat (or was). She is about to learn a lesson!

Practicing for Halloween

"Boo boo, poo poo, ba, ba, nah, nah nah nah…" this was Chloe's chant and rang in Boo's ears on Halloween when the witches and Pirates and Goblins were turned loose to visit the house where Boo lived. Oh, what a frightful night this always was and how afraid Boo was of all these wild raucous children. It was her secret, but she did not like Halloween!

But before the night was over, dear Boo learned a lesson in courage.

Remember two things, reading forward: 1) Boo is a black scaredy cat, who will jump WAYYYY before she is poked! And 2) Her person is a beautiful young teen named Chloe, or as she thinks of her, "Princess" because Boo heard her mama call her that one night and Boo liked it.

"Boo, boo, poo poo, ba, ba, nah nah nah nah," Chloe chanted to BOO who hid behind the closet door and jumped out when she walked by.

"Ha ha, scared ya," Boo always thought, giggling. She loved scaring others, but she did not Like others scaring her! So, Halloween was a time she had never taken a shine to! She was her, that is all.

Boo had her thing.

"I like the fields," she meowed to the princess, Chloe, one day while they were outside, laying on their backs looking up at the blue skies.

Which sounded a lot like "Meow, meow," to Chloe but strangely enough, she knew exactly what Boo was meowing! Hearts in love think like this…and relate, ya know? They understand each other.

Halloween night was coming, and closer and closer it got. Chloe had a costume which she loved and planned to wear to "go trick or treating". Now going trick or treating meant one thing: Candy.

Chloe's mama said this was the year BOO would earn her keep. She would be her own Black cat, and frighten the children, which meant squeals and laughter and running here and there. All in good fun, of course!

Boo was going to be the star of the show on the farm there.

All along the lane, Chloe and the mama of the house, Shannon, would hide behind the trees and urge BOO to run out and scare the visiting children.

Boo's part in this night was well planned. The only one who did not like the plans was, well, Boo. And let me tell you, Boo was horrified!

"I am horrified," She meowed to the Princess, but the Princess laughed excitedly. She patted Boo on the head.

"I am not doing this," Boo meowed to the mama of the house, Shannon. The mama smiled and said, "Try it, you will like it."

The daddy of the house, A Viking named Jon, said, "Leave that cat alone!" Chloe practiced looking at herself in the mirror, wearing her Halloween costume. She looked like a young witch, and she Loved it. She liked to dress up and all the drama and excitement of costumes!

16

See the photo below:

Costume!

Boo watched from the open closet door and now and then she put on her own show. "I may as well practice!" she thought. And she would try hard to act scary! She arched her back, and the princess shouted, "Oh! You scare me!" And then she laughed! And Boo smiled and darted beneath the bed.

Sometimes, Boo found a way to climb up on the roof and she stayed there, hanging her paws over the edges, meowing loudly, until she either fell off (always landed on her feet) and or someone squealed, ran and got a ladder and climbed up and rescued her! Ha ha, ha, that was always fun.

18

She practiced arching her back and looking scary a lot, just in case. You never knew when she might surprise someone, in the shower, waking up early of a morning, or coming in late at night. The arched back always worked great for her.

Sometimes Boo would slip out from beneath the couch while the Princess watched television and show her fangs and meow, "I'll eat you up girl!"

"See how scary I am?"

And the Princess giggled more!

The Princess always giggled which suited Boo just fine. Scaring the princess was a piece of cake!

But she had never succeeded in scaring others because she stayed in the house. She did not scare rabbits. She did not scare birds. She did not scare the moon.

But all that scared her!

Now here it was the dreadful night she was afraid of…Halloween.

How would poor BOO scare anyone when she was secretly afraid of her own shadow?

She liked the idea of Halloween, the tinkling laughter, and children's voices.

She liked dressing up, as the Princess was always dressing her up in wild clothes. Or as we say at Halloween, dressing up in "costumes" which was having fun! Pretending!

Boo liked that part. She just didn't like the....er, dark!!! She was an indoor fur baby and she liked it fine.

She knew the rooms and décor, what might--ha ha--topple over easy and what might not! She slept on any bed she wanted to. She ate all she wanted and if she didn't want what they offered, she just turned up her little nose and walked off!

She pushed and pulled and picked at the nice furniture and kept her claws sharp and ready!

Halloween Arrives!

The mama of the farmhouse, Shannon, put on her costume, as did the dad, Viking Jon. Their faces were, well, scary! Look at the mama, Shannon!

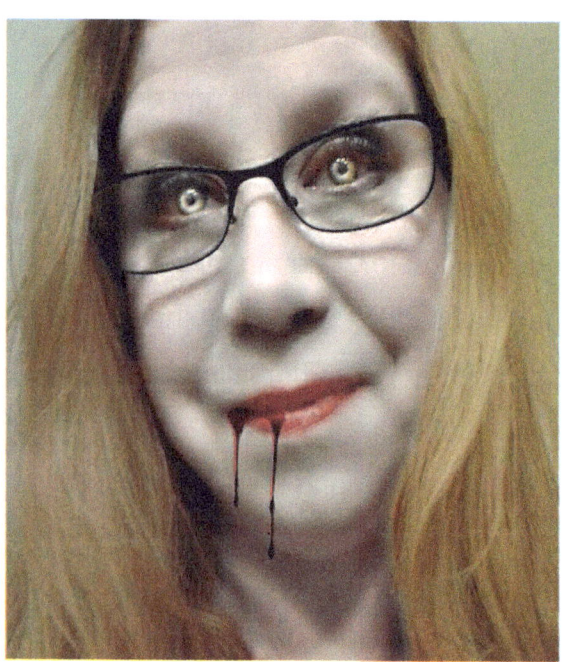

Look at the Princess, Chloe:

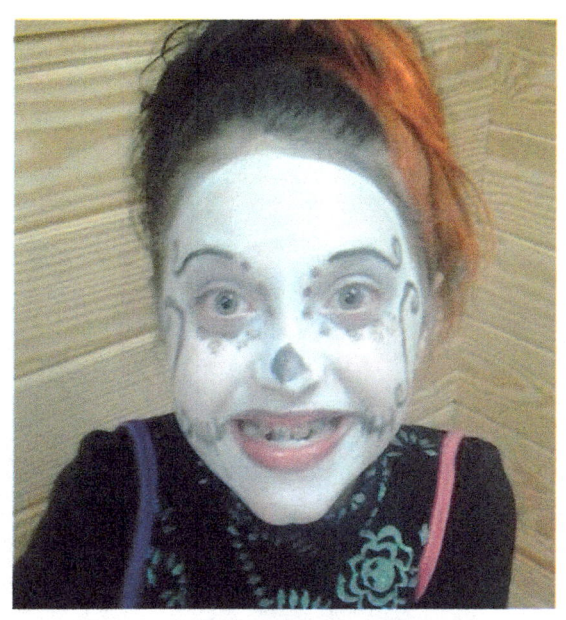

Princess Chloe loved Halloween from the time she was small, and her mama had dressed her up as a pumpkin!

Viking Jon also got into the act. He dressed like a Viking! The children loved it, but not as much as Viking Jon!

25

And of course, BOO was supposed to go as "you are" so to speak, as herself, a black scaredy Cat!

Now here it was, the night of Halloween in late October. Still warm and there was lots of preparations taking place in the farmhouse! Candy was tossed into a huge black caldron, ya know, like a witch's big soup pot or bucket! And this was set outside.

"Boo, boo, poo, poo, ba, ba, nah, nah, nah, nah!" shouted the Princess every time Boo came into the kitchen to see what was going on. Everyone was dressed in their costumes and ready for the visiting children. Ya know, the Trick or Treaters, a noisy bunch but happy!

The farmhouse was down a long dirt lane. On either side was a wooden fence. At the edge of the field was a forest of pine trees (remember?) and it was getting dark outside.

Halloween Decorations

The mama of the house, and the Princess, had hung lanterns along the walkway to the house...on the posts of the fence. The autumn breeze caused the lights to swing slightly, enough to make them flicker and wobble a tad.

All this was outside, remember. It was dark except for the lanterns, so yep, scary as all get out. Spook City!

Along the lane, before the fence posts and the fence, the Princess had made signs and nailed them to sticks. She had stuck these signs into the ground resembling a graveyard.

The Princess had drawn the signs, printed on white posters with a wide tip black magic marker, and the signs were spooky. They took the cake, thought Boo as she trailed along now, behind the Princess and viewed the signs.

The signs looked like monuments found at graves in the cemetery, a mile to the north of here.

One of the signs, rustling a bit in the breeze, read: "Here likes Pete, who died with smelly feet. Boots with him, he is on his last stink!"

One of the signs said, "Here likes Miss Eunice, she was the neighborhood nose…smell that?"

"RIP." Was on one sign, and "Billy was willy nilly and so, ran off the road one dark night and he ain't comin' back!"

One sign, a white poster with black markings and big letters, read:

"RIP Harold the Ripper who wore jeans with holes in them and ripped up everything in sight. With his teeth!"

A sign painted on an old brown board read this:

"Trick or treat, Smell my feet!'

Another sign had a photo of a skeleton trying to climb back up, out of a grave, in the hard earth. The sign beside it had an arrow pointing to it that read, "Viking Jon, came from a world beyond, with slime and crime and not a dime!"

One sign nearby had a photo of animals holding their heads in their paws and rolling their eyes! The eyes bobbed and rolled around. Fishy eyes!

Boo loved to pat and bob ping, pow, bing, bop, those eyes. Once she had knocked an eyeball loose and had to run and secretly glue it back. That one eye was never right again, but no one noticed!

Along the fence line on both sides of the lane leading to the farmhouse were signs on sticks. They were like those "Vote for Me" signs but remember what they said, RIP and messages about the dead people! Ooh lah lah, scary as all get out! The signs were at the head of what appeared to be old graves. The Princess had made these from pebbles and old rugs and blocks, very real looking! She had also used hay bales, stacked one on top of the other!

This whole family loved Halloween and even the mama of the House, was fond of telling everyone how her own granny had loved Halloween and kept her costume hanging in a closet, easy to reach. She always wore an orange wig which the mama of the house thought great!

Boo darted up and down the lane patting some of the signs, batting some of the spider webs the Princess had fashioned out of cotton and draped over the signs and make-shift graves.

The Princess had attached small black spiders and some she had spray painted white into the cobwebs and laid them around on the pretend graves.

Collecting Spiders!

Boo collected as many spiders as she could and ran back and forth, back, and forth up the hill, into the farmhouse and hid the plastic spiders under the bed. There would come a time when she would scare the living daylights out of the Princess but right now, she was mind-blown at all the decorations. Black pumpkins were everywhere, spiders, signs, graves…It gave Boo the creeps if

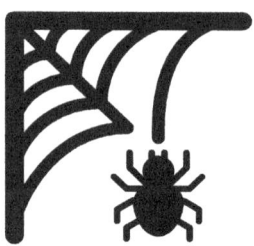

you must know!

35

In the field over the fence was a cotton field of snow-white cotton…this was the time of year for the cotton to ripen and the daddy of the farmhouse, Jon did love to work in cotton. He had, however and for this Halloween night parked his oldest tractor which was named "Lightning" beside the fence so visiting children (later) could see it and get the idea that it was a "dead" tractor!

The tractor was somewhat rusted in spots and the rubber had long ago peeled off the pedals and Boo knew that if monsters existed in those piney woods, which he was sure that they did, they were at least as big as the old tractor.

Poor tractor!

This is the dead tractor, RIP old boy, you plowed many a field! Now driven by the ghost of BD…(who?)

To Boo, the tractor had eyes and those eyes came to her sometimes in a

Nightmare, in which the tractor was cranked up and running wildly, with no one driving it, tearing up the fields and mowing down trees and bushes.

This old tractor, which was ancient and had once upon a summer, caught fire and had to be dragged from the field by a pair of donkeys, oh oh, get ready, this tractor was the scariest decoration of all. Look at those eyes!

But all in all, if you love Halloween you gotta love dead tractors, right? You gotta have nightmares about something!

Back to the House (yay!)

Boo followed the Princess to the end of the lane, darting into the trees now and then but mainly following at the Princess's boots. No sense in getting lost, now what good would that do anyone? Boo stayed close.

"Boo!" shouted the Princess. "Was that an owl in the trees, watching us?" and the Princess picked Boo up and held her in her apron that she wore. She hurried back toward the house. She walked along the winding lane.

At the end of the driveway, between the fence posts, a hayride wagon pulled up, packed with kids of all ages and shapes and sizes. It was this group, in the photo below.

They wore costumes to beat the band! Scary monster masks, some handmade by their mamas and grandmamas!

They were dressed in long dresses, sheets and large shirts, capes and socks and shoes! They laughed and cavorted. They pushed and nudged each other.

They screamed! They squealed.

They jumped down from the hayride wagon and ran helter-skelter up the lane toward the house where Boo lived.

The children were all sizes and on every face was a great smile. They loved having fun, all children love having fun! And these were ready for Trick or Treating adventures.

Good clean fun where nobody gets hurt and or loses (too bad) is always an adventure. Fun on Halloween for this age group was always anticipated and enjoyed. It was a time to remember!

Now remember, Halloween is a fun holiday for all ages, not just children, but mainly children, ok. Everybody loves Halloween that loves Halloween!

Except for fur babies. A lot of fur babies, especially indoor fur babies who don't like for "things" to jump out at them, like odd prints on curtains, fake mice, toys with batteries, bats, blood dripping from a person's mouth, knock-knocking in the night, storms, spiders crawling on your leg, frogs jumping on you, or lizards popping their heads out of your sleeve…all these things, fur babies do not cotton to!

Children Love Halloween!

But yes, I'd say children love this holiday because they love pumpkins, candy and dressing wild and crazy. They like wearing monster masks but not virus masks and bandages on skinned knees.

An example, and a good one, is the photo below of some of the Princess Chloe's cousins, in fact her granny is also in this picture on the front row, left, right in front of her cousin, Joan. The author of this book, Miss Peggy, is in the middle and their cousin, Donna, is on the right.

The boys in this picture (all country kids, mind you) were mean as snakes. In fact, one of them was holding a king snake and if you watch this picture long enough, the snake just MIGHT jump out at ya.

These children in this picture ran all over the woods and their mamas often said, "Be home before dark," because, in the country where they lived, in old farmhouses down a dirt road, there were few Kid laws and few kid baby-sitters. The children were their own babysitters, and the big brothers and sisters' jobs were, watch out for the little ones. Which mean, it was a miracle they all made it to grown up stages.

However, we all know children are a gift from our Father in Heaven, so be it. It is what it is. Some are country children and just free as a summer breeze!

At any rate, the kids in this photo loved Halloween. They did their part, screaming and running here and yon and acting scared when they had to.

They scared Boo half to death. They were always up to something, and she was always on her paws when they came around. They were country children and although Boo was a country cat and had surely experienced her share of accidents and plain misfortunes,
she had never quite seen the energy exhibited by these children! They had attitude! They were pranksters and wild!

Here they are, from all over the river woods, with their baskets, containers, sacks, and boxes. They could hardly wait to trick or treat the mama of this big old farmhouse for she always had the best candy. And whole candy bars at that!

These kids were neighbors and lived in farmhouses, rode horses, mules and canoed in the rivers. They were all stars in the children's book, **The Wild Adventures of Faithy** (which is on Amazon, and I hope you will read it!) because these kids were little outlaws, I tell ya!

Don't they look cute and ready for Halloween? They loved Halloween and I will tell you a secret, next Halloween I will write a book about how they went trick or treating as teenagers and wore football helmets! LOL.

The Princess Takes a Tumble!

The Princess ran ahead, and the children who had just hopped down off the hayride wagon chased her! They yelled stop, stop!

I am telling you these kids were excited about Halloween! They loved playing pranks!

The Princess held Boo tight and close to her, and suddenly her boot caught a stone and she fell head-first into the bushes. She lay there moaning!

Boo hid behind her back and peeked out, blending with the fast-falling darkness! Her eyes sparkled gold!

In the light of the lanterns hanging from the fence posts, Boo's eyes appeared as gold glimmering stones. He watched!

The Princess half-laughed and half-groaned! "Arggggg," she shouted.

Boo's fur stood up on his back big time! He was scared out of his wits!

The children ran up to the Princess, whom they knew well, and began yelling. (All in good fun!) They laughed as they yelled and waved their hands in the air and giggled like a whirlwind grunting!

"Stay there, ya witch's daughter!"

"Loop de loop, you fell in goop!"

"Stiches for witches!"

"RIP witch of the woods!"

And although the friends seemed to be pushing and pulling at the Princess trying to help her get back up again, it looked to Boo as though they were attacking her!

Her black cat blood boiled! She felt herself burst into flames of fright! Boo's sharp claws popped out like swords!

The Princess cried loudly, hoping the tricksters, er, treating kids would move along and leave her alone!

Boo was determined to save the Princess! She was as ready to save her person, the Princess as anything she had ever been. She was not a cat who would fight you, she was not a meanie.

But Boo had been raised by the Princess to love others and "**Do Small things with Great love!**"

This was one of the Princess's favorite sayings. She had raised Boo to love and show kindness. But she had also raised Boo to fight and defend herself if the occasion arose. Like now! She had raised Boo to not allow anyone, anytime, anywhere to bully her, or hit, or talk ugly to her.

"Stand up and fight," the Princess had taught Boo.

"Don't let anyone push you around!' the Princess told Boo often.

And the kids were screaming, and Boo had to fight team fight!

53

"Boo's got fangs!" one kid yelled!

Boo Saves the Princess!

"Nooooo!" Meowed Boo, arching her back and hissing like only black cats can do when frightened! "Yeowsie, mousie, wowsie, my song, you hooligans be gone!" Boo meowed! She hissed bigly.

With her back arched and her fangs barred, making noises deep in her throat, she saw herself fighting a tiger perhaps. Much bigger than Boo!

Or a huge monster, such as King Kong, which she watched on television, with the Princess. Or the Hulk!

Suddenly Boo arched her back and the fur on her oil black, slick shimmering (because the Princess had sprinkled her with glitter of course) coat stood inches above her back! She looked fierce!

"Boo, boo, we ain't scared of you!" said one of the boys dressed in a jailbird's costume with stripes down the sides of his pants, and he ran around Boo and on toward the house.

The other children darted around Boo and headed up the winding lane toward the house. Candy or bust!

Boo stood on her hind legs and scratched at the air behind the children's backs! She hissed and fought the dark night around her! She chased after the children, a few steps only, then ran back to her precious Princess Chloe.

She arched her back and hopped like a rabbit, so fearsome and mad!

Boo's heart revved! It beat faster than a fish flopping on the riverbank. Thump, thump, thump! Kallump, gallump! The fur on her back began calming down. Fighting was a job!

Boo patted the Princess on the cheeks, and she smiled and laughed. Boo climbed into her lap, and she hugged her. Boo licked her jaw.

"You did great! said the Princess and Boo licked her on the hand. The Princess stood up, holding Boo, and walked slowly up the winding lane toward the farmhouse. Her knees were scraped! And she cried softly, sniffling now and then.

The mama sat on the porch singing a witchy sounding song, "Stirring this witch's brew, I'm gonna eat you!" She saw the Princess crying and said, "If you don't stop crying, I'll give you something to cry about!" This was something the mama of the farmhouse had heard her own mama say, many times, and it was something she and the Princess laughed about. Unless she meant beeswax!

Which made the Princess laugh and stop crying! She knew when to stop, for sure. Time to girl up! Cat up!

Boo was so happy the Princess stopped crying. She could hardly bear to hear the Princess weep. It broke her heart for her beloved girl!

The Princess sat Boo down on the steps. The princess told the mama of the farmhouse, who was dressed like a wicked witch, all about how she, the Princess had fallen and scraped her knees. "They called me names, but Boo saved me! You should have seen Boo!"

"I can see! Just not in the dark," laughed the mama. And added, "If you play games, you sometimes tumble and fall. Don't cry like a baby, and if you do don't let anyone see ya!"

Viking Jon Raised from the Dead!

Now, there's more fright!

In the one little square area of grass (remember the yards were mostly dirt due to chickens scratching all day long, every flower and blade of grass and new bulbs they could rake up and eat!

Chickens must scratch my friends),
And I do declare these chickens scratched up the entire farmhouse yard! They were called Lucy and Ethel. These chickens were (are) hoots.

I think you could say they are more like pets than chickens to lay eggs.

Now Lucy is the darker one and Ethel the lighter one and they eat a lot, chase away snakes from the yard and pretty much eat every flower and plant and bulb the mama of the farmhouse, Shannon tries to plant.

I can also tell you for a fact because these chicks are known far and wide as the Bosses. They get away with murdering gnats, ants, or anything else that dares cross their path. There are other chickens here also, and Boo chases them all around the yard.

Back to why I tell you this.

They keep the yard like a beach, which suits these country people just find because the love to go to the ocean. The yard reminds them of sand and sea.

Here are the chickens, Lucy, and Ethel, and I promise you up front these chickens are real, alive, and well, right now, today, scratching and clucking. These are the ones that will peck out your eyes, so Boo loves to chase them. So far, she still has her eyes too.

They don't peck out Boo's eyes because she is faster than a speeding train when she plays with them in the yard. This is the area of grass they leave alone, for some unknown reason.

She gives them a peck for their money and sometimes she has them squawking. Cats love to chase chickens!

Lucy and Ethel!

Boo loves the chickens because they run from her but back to the fact of the yard being bare as a dead animal carcass on a red clay riverbank.

The yard was bare. Except for this one spot where it was grassy. A favorite spot come Halloween!

Of course, the Princess had strung up cotton and spidery web looking strings from one corner of the porch to the other.

Now, see it if you close your eyes. No grass except for this one strip over to the side of the porch where somehow or another, the chickens did not mess with.

And it was on this piece of grass, that the daddy of the farmhouse, Viking Jon was pretending to be a dead man coming out of the dirt!

Viking Jon loved Halloween also, remember I said the entire family had always loved this Holiday.

Like I told you already, the daddy Jon or Viking Jon as he liked being called, dressed as a Viking, which you can look Viking up in the Encyclopedia and it doesn't take a rocket scientist to figure out why he loved playing the part of a Viking.

Viking were awesome dudes!

Vikings were fearless warriors, and it is a known fact they were good students of learning, especially when it came to being fierce and always tall.

Boo loved it when the daddy of the farmhouse, Jon, put on his Viking suit. When others aggravated Boo, Viking Jon always yelled, "Don't mess with that cat!" And Boo felt smug as she pranced away and sat on Viking Jon's knee for safety.

So, Viking Jon, you might say, was a prankster and a good one.

Check out his picture below. A sight for sore eyes and one Boo loved…when Viking Jon was like this, sometimes, Boo would run over and slap him on the head, then dash off. She loved it! He laughed. It always scares kids when they see…

A dead man raising himself up from what appears to be a grave!

Hand and feet bones.

A Viking going, "Ayyyyy!"

Or growling and slobbering like a run mad dog!

Look at the picture. This is Viking Jon and isn't he scary!

He acts like he is having fun, which he is! Sometimes Boo would drag the hands and feet away. In fun!

Boo Finds her Way Inside the House!

Boo ran through the front door and climbed up on the couch and stared through the window at the children, grabbing candy from the mama. What a sight for sore eyes! But she was safe, on the back of her wonderful smelly, scratched up cat couch! She stopped shaking! Whew, close call!

The Princess came inside and stood at the couch with Boo.

"Thank you Boo, I love you!" the Princess said.

"You saved my life, gallant lady!"

And then she chanted softly, "Boo, boo, poo poo, ba ba, nah, nah, nah, nah!"

And Boo jumped down and hid in the closet! Then out again and jumped onto the couch. Then back, then back!

The night grew darker, and the full moon shone like a light from the sky high above. The wind howled. Halloween was here and it would pass because she had heard Viking Jon say, 'This too shall pass!"

And Boo could see through the window how the daddy of the house, Viking Jon, was still laying in the spot of grass.

The chicken, Lucy, walked over and pecked his toes. Ouch!

The Princess left the room and went back outside. She squealed and laughed and swapped whole candy bars with the visiting children. Boo watched from inside the house, sitting on the back of the couch. She liked being safe!

The children as well as the Princess had a great time, running up and down the lane. Squealing, acting horrified!

Only the black cat, Boo, knew for sure there were ghosts out there, in the forests of pines and oak trees, as well as panthers as big as tractor tires and monsters like…like…who knew?

The Truth About Boo

When she was a baby just a few weeks old, a tiny kitten, Boo had been accidentally lost in the forest and left behind by others of her family. Now see if you can picture her, big as a sock maybe, or perhaps a tennis ball and as black as the midnight hour. Just little bitty!

She meowed loudly all night until the next morning, cold and horrified she hid inside an old pipe.

She was weak and terrified and on the verge of giving up hope. Her little eyes were puffy from crying tears of heart break.

She shivered from fear! She thought she was a goner for sure. She cried her little eyes out! She sniffled and hid in the leaves. A tiny little ball of innocent fur!

The Princess, walking down the lane to wait for the yellow school bus, at the end of the lane, on the old dirt road that passed by the farmhouse, miraculously heard Boo's cries.

"What is that?" she asked the pine trees and the briar brush and the field of white cotton beyond the trees.

Of course, the forest answered! Because see, the Princess loved the forest and the forest loved her!

And when you speak the earth's secret language, it will answer you!

The yellow school bus pulled up to the bus stop and opened its doors. The school bus driver was a guy named Phillip who wore a baseball cap and read books to the children every time the bus stopped. Today, he was reading the Bible.

"I am not going today! I've got to save an animal!" The Princess yelled, and the yellow bus pulled off and left her in a cloud of red field dust!

The Princess ran into the woods, hidden by tall pine trees, scratchy briar bushes and sweet-smelling honeysuckle vines.

She searched everywhere, behind stumps and under fallen trees.

She followed the weak, whimpering cries of the lost fur baby! Finally, she found the old pipe, and without blinking, having no fear, the Princess knelt and crawled halfway into the huge pipe and then reached her arm long and pulled tiny little Boo out by her matted fur.

She saw a red-tailed hawk flying by, overhead, searching for food and the Princess knew she had rescued the fur baby just in the nick of time. She wept tears of joy and cuddled the tiny kitten.

She was a little bitty, pitiful baby kitten, but the Princess loved her at first sight! She called her Boo!

The Princess rushed back to the farmhouse and yelled for her mama, who loved kittens above and beyond measure.

The mama of the House, Shannon, took Boo in and together, they gave her a warm bath, milk in a bowl to drink and a blanket to wrap up in (and hide).

Boo hid all day, waiting for the Princess to come home. For the daddy of the house, had driven the Princess to school after all, and so, she was in school like it or not!

Boo heard the bus driving down the lane and in the mama's overalls pocket, they hurried down the lane to the bus stop!

Boo peeped all around, and when the Princess saw her little black head peeking from the pocket of her own mama's overalls, she cried and said, "Boo!"

The Princess cried and Boo's little, tiny heart filled with joy and of course, never-ending love.

The Princess took Boo in her arms and carried her back to the house where Boo was loved and taken care of for the rest of her life.

And just so you know, Boo had been found the day after a scary Halloween night long ago, in the woods, down the old dirt road, so she knew the woods were full of monsters on Halloween night.

And no, for many years Boo never did like Halloween, but she got through it and when the occasion came about, Boo was able to scare when scaring was called for. She stepped up!

And that was Halloween night here and now. She had just learned that Halloween was a hair-raising fun night, and all was well. No monsters the size of the old red tractor tires, had eaten her or gobbled her up, as they say. The event was just plain fun! Kind of!

She had come to the rescue of the Princess, indeed, and it had given her courage!

She had not let her fear stop her, and when the Princess fell down Boo was right there to save her. Because remember, the Princess had once upon a time, long ago, saved Boo.

And it wasn't so bad after all. "Stand up," Boo's inner voice had said to her. "Show up, do what is right!"

Be you. Be like Boo!

Boo had found out Fear was not the big old Monster she had thought it was. And would never be. It was like a stone at the creek, something to pick up and throw back.

Facing her fear on the road when the Princess fell, called for bravery and Boo was very proud of herself for showing No fear. For showing bravery. Bravery feels good! Bravery is easy!

Sure, she was afraid. Boo came into this world afraid, especially when she was so tiny and close to hopeless, lost in that big old forest full of shadows and horrible noises.

But her courage gave her power from on High. She was born to be brave, even on Halloween! She had found hope when she was rescued by the Princess!

And she would also choose to be brave and love others. Especially those who loved her the most.

She loved her Princess and always would be there for her. She was her person and Boo was her cuddle bug and her pillow and her companion and there is nothing in this world as wonderful as a fur baby on lonesome nights.

This is the truth about Boo, and about your fur babies too. Stars in your lives, which create love and courage!

This my friends, is the Truth about Boo. Don't you love true stories?

81

Boo's Mottos, As Learned from the Princess:

"When you run out of options, remember to be brave!"

"Fear is like a biscuit you have hidden. After while it dries out and crumbles."

"Be you. Be like Boo!'

**Have fun on Halloween, it's just one night!"

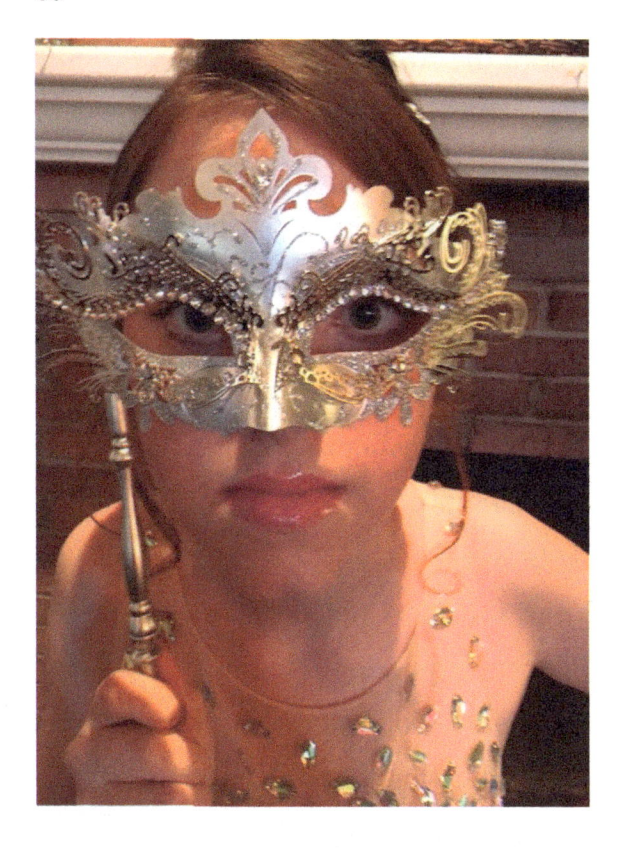

The end, and Happy Halloween, from the Princess Chloe, Boo, and the family!

About the Author

Peggy Mercer is a Georgia author who has been making up her own stories since she was four years old. She first learned to write her name, in cursive, on old farmhouse walls at the Adams place, near the Satilla River, her favorite place in the world (where she fished, standing on a stump!).

She won **Georgia Author of the Year, in 2011** for a children's book, **Peach, When the Well Run Dry** and **Georgia Independent Author of the Year, 2021** for a novel, **Another Island, Another Moon.**

She has worked as a teacher, songwriter, Poet and ghostwriter for a major television contributor, and lives in the woods in Georgia.

www.peggymercerworldwide.org

Other award-winning children's books by Peggy Mercer include: Ga. Author of The Year in 2011 or GAYA in Atlanta, Georgia. **Peach, When the Well Run Dry** published by Marimba Books, NY. Wade Hudson, Editor. The book is about friendship between a young boy and an old water diviner, in a time of drought, based on a true story, set in the South and near Axson, Georgia.

87

There Come a Soldier, with art by world known, Ron Mazellan. Published by Handprint-Chronicle Books, NY., and San Diego.

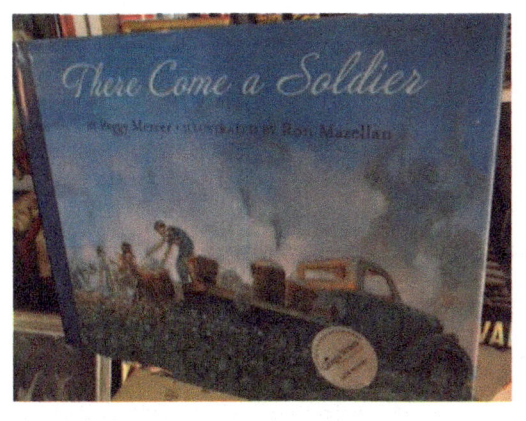

Award winning books by this author:

Ten Cows to Texas, published by Handprint-Chronicle Books, Ny, Ny with full pages of colorful illustrations, ages 5 and up.

The Wild Adventures of Faithy, published by Wilson Publishing Company, Florida. Early reader with chapters. Ages 6-10

Moaf Cried Ghost, a Halloween book created for and used by a gifted program in a public school. Ages 6-9

The Crazy Stories about a YA who is mentally disturbed, rather humorous stories based on real characters and introduced by a California psychiatrist, Dr. Trey Meeks.

News and Reviews!

Peggy Mercer is creating a major podcast on writing, to help aspiring writers, called **The Writing Masterclass: Writing for Love and Money**. Please visit her website and tune in as soon as the podcast launches. You will learn how to do this! You will learn how to write your own stories.

Please visit my Author Page on **Amazon** and check out my other books on my Amazon site.

And if your child enjoys this book, please contribute by writing a great 5-star review on Amazon, as every review will help!

Write me a note if you loved this book, as I love to hear from my young readers and I will write back!

**Peggy Mercer
988 Estlee Mercer Road
Douglas, Ga. 31535**

One of my most beautiful, and favorite Sunday School students of all time, Lori Smith McBride, wrote to me the other day that she had kept a note I had written to her when she was a child and the note said, "Be faithful in the small things…" I love that story, as this lady is a grandmother now! I hope I have influenced children with great love! I know that she is influencing her own family with her beautiful smile and great love.

You may also donate to my writing by mailing me a check. Many of my books are donated freely to underserved children and schools rebuilding from disasters.

Award Winning Author Peggy Mercer

Grew Up Loving Elvis

-Poetry-

"Congrats and success to you for making life meaningful as an author. Your books are inspiring!"
-Taylor Swift

I recently was able to donate books to schools in New Orleans, Louisiana, that are rebuilding due to flooding disasters. My private foundation, "Give a Child a book and a Chance" is made possible by kind readers donating!

For young Readers who want to write their own stories, read on....

I included in this book, a guide for you to use, to create your very own story!

Get read to write your own tall tales! You can do this!

Write Your own Story using the following literary elements:

1. Decide who your main character will be. Describe him or her.

If you have trouble deciding on a character think of yourself and make this "star" of the story much like yourself. This way you will be able to share your own feelings of love, hope, excitement, and the way you look at a certain problem, school, grades, friends, adults.

2. Starting point. Give your main character a place to start or jump into the deep of the story.

Start your story where it starts. As we say, "Just tell the story!"

Don't tell too much to start with, save the parts of the story that fatten the story up for later.

Remember to use your main facts, such as Who the story is about, what they are doing or facing (their issue or problem they must overcome), Where is the story taking place. When is the story taking place and if possible, talk about the why!

3. Identify your character's challenge of problem that he or she must overcome.

In every story, the character of "star" of the story has a problem he or she must solve. How does he or she go about this, I would suggest that you plot the story out, or do what we call an outline.

Outlines are wonderful. Mention all the important points of the story that your character must reach or get to, to move the story action forward.

Don't get off track. Stay focused! Don't waste words!

4. Give your story what we call rising action, leading to the main event or peak of the story. (Climax)

What does your character say, tell the dialogue and make it sound authentic! How do the characters really speak to each other? Use that! Don't worry about being proper. Just talk between the people.

Show the action, don't necessarily tell it. Show action, rather than fat paragraphs!

Every word you use in your talking, every step they take must be important and move your story forward. This is what we call action!

5. Climax or high point of the story.

Show the reader the high point of the story or the center HAPPENING...that is the top of the story mountain! Action moves toward this peak or story climax since you began your story. I always know my climax in advance and have it on my outline, so it doesn't startle me (too much).

The high point to me is when the reader gets struck by the story lightning, now it might surprise the reader or make them panic, or happy beyond words. But it will strike them!

6. Falling action.

The action, after the climax or peak will begin to go downhill and become calmer. It will be like riding a bike down hill or down a quiet street. This is the part of the story where everything levels off and begins to rush or walk slowly toward the end of the story.

Every story must end...Sigh. That is what I love so much about stories. They have three parts, a beginning, a middle and an end. And always remember there are stories you will never, ever forget. I hope you write one someday!

7. Tie a BOW…tie the story up with finished ideas or confluence…THE END will be the result. Readers want to know what happens to the main character and any other characters you have introduced in your story. Don't leave the reader wondering! Tell them what happens to the characters and make them happy. Nobody likes sad endings!

Invitation:

Now I invite you to go back and read this book again and again and enjoy it forevermore. Your friend, Miss Peggy Mercer loves you!

These are the neighbor's donkey's who watched this whole Halloween story unfold. They knew the Truth About Boo was a true story.

"Children who *READ* are given a set of *KEYS*... these are the *KEYS* to all of *LIFE*...everything they can ever want and need, they can find in #BOOKS....for *Books are Keys.*"

Peggy Mercer (c) 2018

> "Authors must write themselves ragged..."
> -Peggy Mercer

Authors must write while others loaf. You must write while other's fish and look around at the stuff of life. Authors must outline and then stay at it, until you can write "The End" on the tale you are composing. If you have a desire to become an author, you need to know up front that it is hard work. It is like a wheel, it just keeps on turning but only if you roll with it.

Give a

Child a

Book

And a

Chance

Private Foundation
(Gacabac)
Peggy Mercer

PayPalMe/PeggyMercerWorldwide

Thank you, readers, for reading this book, I hope to see you again soon. I am currently writing a book about a bully, and a series for girls and boys!

Made in the USA
Columbia, SC
25 August 2023